SEAGULL B
The Story o

SMITHSONIAN OCEANIC COLLECTION

For Libby and Henry, with love from your Nini. With special thanks and tremendous love to J.B.—V.G.B.

For my dear friends, Hayden and Olivia Reeder—A.L.

Book copyright © 2011 Palm Publishing, LLC, 353 Main Avenue, Norwalk, CT 06851, and the Smithsonian Institution, Washington, DC 20560.

Published by Soundprints, an imprint of Palm Publishing, LLC, Norwalk, Connecticut.
www.soundprints.com

Editor: Laura Gates Galvin   **Series design:** Shields & Partners, Westport, CT
Book layout: Colleen Towne   **Production coordinator:** Chris Dobias   **Audio design:** Laura Gates Galvin

First Edition 2011
10 9 8 7 6 5 4 3 2 1
Printed in China

Acknowledgments:
   Our very special thanks to Marcy Heacker of the Feather Identification Lab at the Smithsonian Institution's National Museum of Natural History for her curatorial review.
   Soundprints would also like to thank Ellen Nanney and Kealy Wilson at the Smithsonian Institution's Office of Product Development and Licensing for their help in the creation of this book.

Library of Congress Cataloging-in-Publication Data is on file with the publisher and the Library of Congress.

SEAGULL BY THE SHORE
The Story of a Herring Gull

by Vanessa Giancamilli Birch   Illustrated by Alton Langford

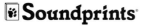

It is a warm May afternoon along the Atlantic Ocean seashore and the sun is shining brightly. A lobster scuttles along the ocean floor looking for its meal, and on the surface of the water, a Seagull bobs up and down with the waves. She is a Herring Gull. The ocean is still cold from the long winter, but the cold water doesn't bother Seagull. Her white head floats up and down in the choppy ocean.

Soon it will be time for Seagull to start a family. She needs to find a mate who will help her build a nest where she can lay eggs, and once the eggs hatch, help her raise the chicks.

Seagull flies out of the ocean and lands on the sandy beach. She takes a few steps, walking closer to the ocean and then runs away from the waves as they crash onto the shore. She waddles along the shoreline, picking through the seaweed, shells and sticks that the waves leave behind. She is looking for something to eat.

Seagull spots a male gull flying above her. The male gull holds a clam in his bill, which he drops onto the boardwalk near her, hoping to crack its shell and give Seagull something to eat. This will surely impress Seagull and make her want to choose him as a mate.

But the clam's hard shell doesn't break! The male gull swoops down and picks up the clam in his bill. He drops it on the boardwalk again, and it still doesn't break. Seagull stands nearby, watching the male gull as he picks up the clam for one last try.

Finally, the clam's tough outer shell breaks open. The male gull lands next to the clam to make sure other birds don't take the food from the cracked shell. He lifts his head and lets out a high-pitched cry, calling for Seagull to join him. Seagull has found a mate!

11

Soon, Seagull and her mate look for a safe, sheltered place to build their nest. They fly to a small island in the ocean that looks free of predators. They travel back and forth from the island to the shore, where they pick up grass, sticks, leaves, pieces of seaweed and even items pulled from trash cans. They line their nest with the material they collect.

After many trips to the shore, Seagull and her mate have made a safe, warm nest. Mother Seagull lays three brown, speckled eggs and sits on them until Father Seagull returns with food. She then leaves the nest to find her own food.

Both parents closely watch the eggs to protect them from harm. One day, while Mother Seagull is off looking for food, Father Seagull spots a crow from where he sits on the nest. He watches as the crow circles the island and swoops down toward the nest, landing on a fallen tree trunk nearby. The crow perches on the log and looks around. Father Seagull tries to hide the eggs by lowering his head and covering them with his wing. The crow takes a few steps toward the nest and then flies away. It was a close call, but Father Seagull and the eggs are safe.

As Mother Seagull walks along the sand looking for food, she spots a trash can overflowing with discarded containers, bottles, beach toys, magazines and newspapers. She perches on the rim of the trash can and peers into it. She uses her big, yellow bill to dig through the trash, looking for something to eat.

Mother Seagull finds the handle of a plastic sand pail. She has never seen anything like this so she nibbles at it, thinking it is food. When she realizes it's not something to eat, she tosses the broken handle back into the heap of trash. She rummages some more and finds a piece of a peanut-butter-and-jelly sandwich. She eats it and flies back to the water.

19

Before going back to the nest, Mother Seagull spends some time floating on the waves, eating small fish and insects swimming near her. She opens her bill and swallows a few gulps of the salty ocean water. She prefers to drink freshwater, but her special glands filter salt from the water so she can drink it safely.

In the early dawn hours, after four weeks of sitting on the eggs to keep them warm, Mother Seagull hears a soft tapping coming from one of the eggs. The egg slowly begins to crack. *Tap, tap, tap. Crack!* Small pieces of the shell fall to the bottom of the nest. The tip of a tiny, black bill pokes out of the crack in the egg. Next a head appears, and then wings and then the chest. The eggs are hatching!

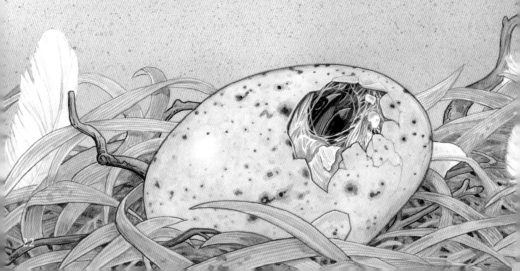

By late morning, all three of the eggs have hatched. Three tiny chicks, covered in soft down, move around the nest, bumping into each other as they begin to open their eyes. By tomorrow, the chicks will be able to move around easily, although they'll stay close to the nest for safety.

But right now, the chicks are hungry! They make begging calls and touch their parents' bills. This is their way of asking for food.

Father Seagull leaves the nest to find food for his babies. He flies to a nearby park where a family is eating a picnic lunch. A young boy drops a piece of bread. Father Seagull swoops down from the sky and snatches the bread from the ground. The little boy squeals with delight as Father Seagull takes off into the bright blue sky to bring the food home to the chicks.

For the next five weeks, Mother and Father Seagull take turns finding small fish, crabs, insects and even scraps of food from a leftover picnic to feed the chicks. Each day, the chicks grow bigger and stronger. The young seagulls begin to venture out of the nest, but they never stray far from it.

29

In July, after two months of caring for the gulls, Mother and Father watch as the chicks begin to fly from the nest to find their own food. Four years from now, they will find mates and have chicks of their own. Once summer is over and the temperature becomes colder, the young gulls will fly to warmer weather. Mother and Father Seagull will stay near the nest they have built until next year, when they will lay more eggs and start a new family.

About the Herring Gull

Herring Gulls (*Larus argentatus*) are birds that spend most of their lives near water—both saltwater and freshwater. They can also be found in man-made places, like garbage dumps or plowed fields. They are common in North America, Central America and Europe, but also can be found in Asia and Russia.

Herring Gulls do not breed until they are four or five years old. They are a monogamous species, meaning one male mates with one female for at least the length of the breeding season, but sometimes for life. Both the male and female Herring Gulls help build the nest, which is typically located on the ground, in a protected location. The female Herring Gull usually lays a group of three eggs called a clutch, but both parents incubate the eggs for nearly a month until the eggs hatch. Herring Gull chicks ask for food from their parents by begging with calls and touching their parents' bills. The chicks leave the nest soon after hatching, but stay near the nest for up to six weeks before they begin to fly and venture out on their own.

The Herring Gull is a common and widespread large seagull. The number of Herring Gulls went down during the 19th Century, when they were hunted for their feathers and eggs. Larger birds, foxes or coyotes have been known to prey on the Herring Gull. Because they nest on the ground, Herring Gull eggs and chicks are in danger of being taken by raccoons, weasels, crows and even other gulls.

Herring Gulls are considered omnivores, which means they will eat many different types of food, such as fish and worms, clams or other mollusks found in the water, but they also may eat small birds, eggs or even human garbage. The birds like to drink freshwater when it is available, but if they have to they will drink saltwater. They have special glands above their eyes that allow them to get rid of the salt and make the saltwater drinkable.

Glossary

lobster: a large marine crustacean that has pincers on its front legs.
clam: an aquatic bivalve mollusk with a hard, two-part shell.
predators: animals that prey on other animals.

freshwater: water without salt, often found in inland lakes and rivers.
bill: a bird's beak.